Dial Books for Young Readers
Penguin Young Readers Group
An imprint of Penguin Random House LLC
375 Hudson Street
New York, NY 10014

Published by Penguin, 2017

Printed in China
9780735227460

10 9 8 7 6 5 4 3 2 1

Text set in Sassoon Sans Std

FlaSh the FiSh

by Paul Kor
translated by Annette Appel

Dial Books for Young Readers

Once upon a time,
deep under the sea,
lived a little fish—
a silver fish called Flash.

Flash had brothers and sisters
and cousins galore.
The family swam together
as if they were one big fish.

Only Flash liked to swim by himself,
faster and farther than the others.

He liked to slice and dive
through the waves,
and greet every fish he met.

Large fish and small fish.
Striped fish and spotted fish.
Even seahorses and jellyfish.

One morning,
Flash swam far, far away.
The sea was quiet and blue.

Suddenly, Flash spied something big and black in the water.
"It must be a mountain," Flash thought.
"What else could it be?"

Carefully, Flash swam a little closer.

And a little closer . . .

In the middle of the big black thing was a great big eye.
An eye that was looking right back at Flash.
And it was crying.

"Oh my," thought Flash. "This isn't a mountain at all.
Mountains do not have eyes,
and they certainly do not cry.
So what can this big black thing be?"

Bold and brave, Flash began to swim
around the thing that was not a mountain.
Beneath the crying eye,
he found a long row of stripes,
like glistening, shimmering ribbons of white.

And from behind the stripes
there came a rumbling voice.
It sounded to Flash like the boom of a thousand drums.

The voice said:

"WHO ARE YOU, LITTLE FISH?".

Flash did two flips in the water.
"Me?" he said. "I'm Flash, a tiny silver fish.
Who are you?"

The voice answered:
"I AM A WHALE."

"Really?" Flash said.
"I've never seen a whale before.
You're so large! All I can see
are some teeth and one big eye."

"Of course that's all you can see.
You're too close," said the whale.
"Go far away and look again."

Flash began to swim away,
but the whale was so big and so wide
that it seemed she would never end.

"Farther!" the whale called.

So Flash swam on and on,

farther and farther . . .

Until finally, he could see the entire whale.

"Wow!" Flash cried out from afar.
"You *are* huge.
But why are you crying?
I thought that's what little babies did."

"I *am* little," the whale sobbed.
"I went for a swim and now I'm lost.
I can't find my mama and papa."

She sobbed loudly, and tear after tear fell from her eyes.

"Don't cry," Flash called.
He swam back to the whale.
"I'll help you.
I'll find your mama and papa.
Okay?"

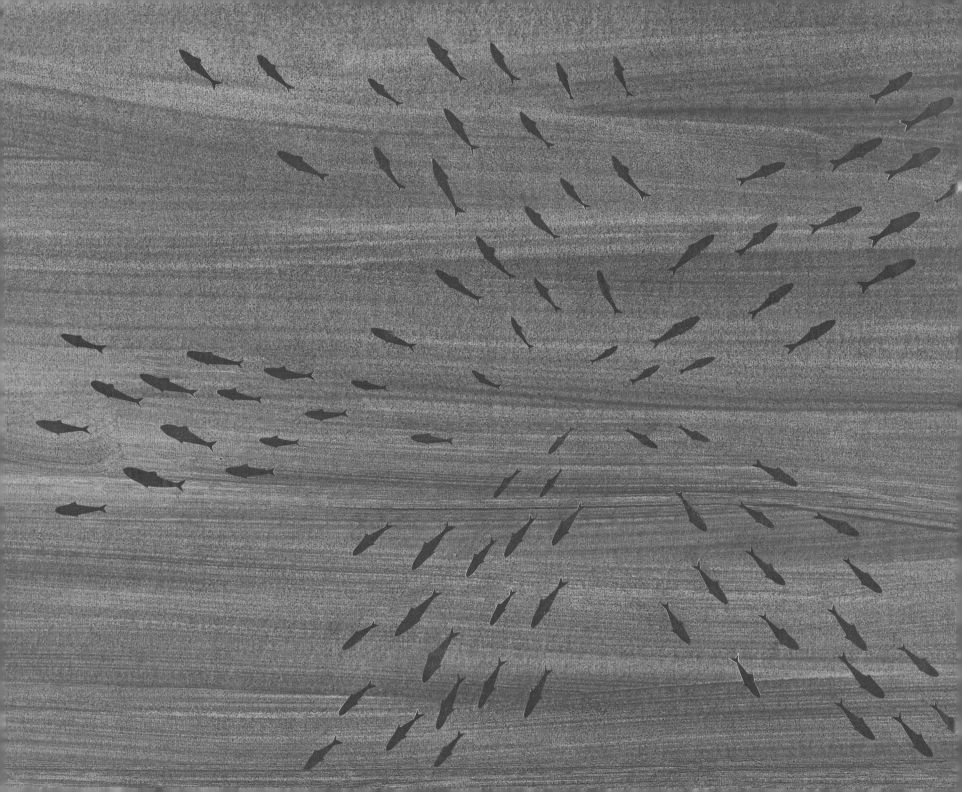

Flash quickly gathered his brothers
and sisters and cousins
to look for Mama and Papa Whale.
Eager to help, the fish rushed out to sea
like sharp silver arrows.

Little Flash stayed back with
his new friend the whale.

"Don't worry," he said.
"We'll find your parents. Just wait and see."

The whale barely had time to wipe her tears
before all the silver fish returned.
And with them—
Mama and Papa Whale!

They were enormous!
Gigantic!
And they were smiling and laughing, happy as can be.

Mama and Papa swam circles around
the little whale and cried out,
"Thank you, thank you,
our dear little Flash!"

The day drew to a close.
Everyone said good night
and swam back home.

Since then, every day,
Flash visits the whale,
and the two of them play in the sea.

Flash is not afraid.
And the whale doesn't cry.

They are the best of friends.